Prince

AND THE

Hot Diggory Dogs

STORMONT
SCHOOL

Also available in Hodder Story Books

Prince Vince and the
Case of the Smelly Goat

Text copyright © Valerie Wilding 1995
Illustrations copyright © Guy Parker-Rees 1995

First published in Great Britain in 1995
by Hodder Children's Books

The right of Valerie Wilding to be identified as the Author of the Work has been asserted by her in accordance with the
Copyright, Designs and Patents Act 1988.

10 9 8 7 6 5 4 3 2 1

A Catalogue record for this book is available from the British Library

ISBN 0340 626542

Printed and bound in Great Britain by
Cox & Wyman Ltd, Reading, Berks.

Hodder Children's Books
A Division of Hodder Headline plc
338 Euston Road
London NW1 3BH

Prince Vince

AND THE

Hot Diggory Dogs

BY VALERIE WILDING

ILLUSTRATED BY GUY PARKER-REES

Hodder
Children's
Books

a division of Hodder Headline plc

For my mother
Rosina Allin
with love.

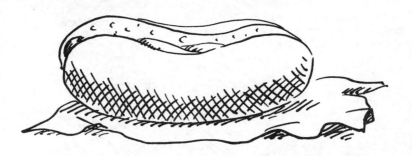

Boom! Boom! Pfoop!

"Why are you hiding, Dad?" Prince Vince asked.

"Boxer's after me." The King slid behind a statue of his great-grandfather Griswold.

Too late.

Captain Boxer spotted him and sprang to attention, nose skywards. "Beg pardon for distarbin' the Royal walking-about, Yer Maje*sty*!" he barked. "Royal Marching Band awaits inspection. *Sah*!"

The King sighed. "On m'way."

"Will His 'ighness be accompanying you? Sah!"

"Of course. Another Royal duty to learn for when he's King."

Vince groaned and trailed his father to a wooden podium, set up beside the gravel drive, like a miniature stage. "*Must* I, Dad?" he moaned. "The band's awful. It's getting worse."

"Quiet, boy, and stay off my podium. You're tall enough without it."

"By the left, qui-hick *march*!" Boxer led the band up the drive; they played the King's own tune, 'The March of Mighty Maximus'.

Boom! Boom! Boom! went the drummer. *Boom! Boom!* Pfoop.

Vince laughed. "He's banged right through the sides."

*BLARR BLARR WAA*aaah! The slide shot off the trombone and clonked the trumpeter in the back of the neck. The cymbal player laughed so much he clashed too hard and broke a cymbal. It rolled like a dropped coin.

Windows slammed shut.

Vince feigned a coughing fit as the band drew
near, and a gardener put a bucket over his
head and waited for the din to die down.

"Eyes - *right*!" Boxer thundered.

The cymbal wheeled full circle and tripped
up the glockenspiel player. *Plink
plinkle plinkle CLONK.* The knob of his beater
flew off and landed in the upturned bell of the
euphonium. *Oom-pah oom-pah oom-pah mmfff.*

8

The band rounded the far corner of the castle, bits dropping off and the odd fist flying. When the only sounds were the crunch of marching feet and the lonely *ting ting ting* of the triangle bringing up the rear, the gardener removed his bucket, windows opened, and Vince wiped his streaming eyes. A guardsman pottered up the drive collecting instrument parts, muttering, "Flipping load of rubbish."

"He's right," Vince said. "They *are* rubbish. Someone should do something."

The King glared. "Oh, do shut up." Macclesfield, the butler, had already served coffee in the Morning Room, grazing his thumb on a chipped saucer. The Queen slapped on a plaster - she always carried one just in case - and sank back with her book.

"At least we know why the band's so awful," said Vince. "That's a relief."

"Stupid boy," the King snapped. "A relief? How?"

"Their playing's OK. All you need do is buy new instruments."

The King fidgeted. "I can't."

"Why?"

"Questions, questions!" The King dunked a garibaldi biscuit. Most of it dropped off and he scalded his finger fishing for it.

"Ow!" he said, "Ow!"

Vince refused to change the subject. "Why can't you buy new instruments?"

"Because there's no money!" the King burst out. "We're broke."

Corks! Dad always had enough to buy a new carriage or fishing rod or to throw huge birthday parties for himself. "Broke?" Vince repeated.

"Not *exactly* – but we can't afford fripperies."

"Hear that, Mum?"

The Queen marked her place with a finger. "What?"

"There's no money for fripperies."

She shrugged. "Don't want no fripperies."

"The band does."

The Queen rolled her eyes. "Yes sirree, they sure need new instruments."

Mum's reading Westerns again, Vince thought. She's talking like a cowboy.

"All *right*," the King snapped. "They do. But I've no cash."

"We'll raise some!" said Vince. "Everyone, think of a way."

Hearing a screechy wail from outside, the King said defensively, "the bagpipes are OK."

Vince went to the window. "That's not bagpipes. It's Larky, singing!"

Larky's voice was famous for its awfulness.

The King exploded. "What the dubbins is a kitchen maid doing in my garden? I don't know, everybody wanders exactly where they like. They think it's open house."

Vince sniggered. "Open castle, more like." He stopped dead. "Hey, I've got it! Let's open the castle to the public. Not *every* day," he added hastily. "Just public holidays, like

Griswold's Day. That's only a few weeks away. People can pay to tour the castle and picnic in the grounds."

"Whoa!" said the Queen. "You ain't got no cause to git carried away, kid."

Vince ignored her. "We'll sell souvenirs with Dad's face on. We'll make heaps of money for instruments, and there'll be loads left over. For fripperies." He nudged the Queen. "Like books."

"Reet good idea, son." She twirled an imaginary lasso in the air. "Yeee-*har*!"

Vince sat back, satisfied. This should be fun.

Vince in Charge

The King refused to discuss the idea until after lunch, then he sent for Boxer.

The Captain saluted and stamped, making the Queen lose her page.

"At ease," said the King. "M'son has an idea."

Vince outlined the Open Day suggestion.

The Captain's nose aimed high. "Most grateful His 'ighness wants to 'elp the band. Owhever," he continued, "me and me men couldn't be doin' with it. *Sah!*"

"Pity," the King said, insincerely.

Vince leapt up, toppling the sauce bottle. A sticky brown trail trickled towards the King. "Ask *why* he can't be doing with it, Dad!"

The King smiled. His elbow was in the sauce, Vince noted with satisfaction.

"Why, Boxer," the King drawled, "can't you be doing with it?"

"Me and me men cannot ensure the safety of the Royal what-nots if riff-raff rampages through the castle. Sah!"

"Quite right," the King snorted as, to Vince's fury and disappointment, he dismissed Boxer, and ambled off for his afternoon nap.

"They're not riff-raff," Vince fumed, "and if Captain Boxer can't cope, I, Prince Vincent Alexandro de Maximus Roy, flipping well can!" He turned to the Queen. "You believe I can, don't you, Mum?" He tapped her book. "Fripperies, remember."

The Queen slapped the table. "No son of mine is gonna be a quitter. Go tell your pa. I'm right behind you."

Vince led her to the Royal Rest Room,

where his father was already snuggled into a King-sized velvet beanbag. Bending down, he whispered, "Dad, let me organise the Open Day. You *know* I can do it. We'll make enough money for instruments; maybe even a new carriage."

A pointed toe kicked him sharply in the rear.

"And books for Mum," he added.

The King stirred. "Mmmff."

"I'll arrange security, too. I won't let you down, Dad. I swear."

"All ri'. Leave me 'lone."

"Say yes, and I will."

"Yesss. Yessss."

Vince hurried the Queen outside. "You heard him. He said I could do it. Didn't he?"

"Sure did, pardner."

He wished she'd go off Westerns.

Vince headed for the kitchen, where the cook offered him a pasty.

"Thanks, Mrs Doughboy. Guess what!"

"What, Prince Vince lovey?"

"We're going to open the castle – to the public!" he explained quickly.

Mrs Doughboy immediately began to fret. "What a lot of mouths to feed! The whole town might come. I'll do sandwiches, scones, Royal Shorties, Castle Cupcakes…"

Her voice was drowned as Larky
approached with a basket of raspberries,
singing at the top of her horrible voice,
　"Raspberries is good for little girlies
　Raspberries is good for little boys
　But the raspberry that's best –
　The one that beats the rest
　Is the raspberry that makes a nasty noise."
　She stuck her tongue out and blew a
thunderous raspberry.

Vince choked with laughter, and made her shut up while he explained his idea. "I promised Dad I'd be responsible for everything – organisation, entertainments – but especially security. The safety of the Royal possessions will be my responsibility and, well, you know what Dad thinks of me."

Larky knew the King thought him worse than useless, and that Vince was desperate to prove otherwise.

"So," he continued, "if I can rely on you, Mrs D, for good food –"

Mrs Doughboy stiffened. "I think you can trust my cooking."

"Oh, *I'll* say." Vince said, hurriedly. "What I meant was I'll leave all the catering to you. And, Mrs D, Larky's pretty sharp-eyed and –"

"You want her to help you?" Mrs Doughboy glared at Larky. "Long as the noisy madam does her proper work first thing each morning –"

Larky kissed her noisily. "Ta!" she bawled.

Mrs Doughboy clapped her hands to her ears. "Go and pick some parsley, girl."

Outside, Vince asked Larky, "Do you think people will come?"

"They'd want to see inside the castle, sure 'nuff." She nodded. "Yeah, if there's plenty to do. Why not book the fair, and a bouncy wotsit, and get people to set up stalls? You can charge a sort of rent for the day." She grinned. "We'll make snoodles of money!"

Vince grinned back. Larky might be noisy and disrespectful, but she was game for anything. Hadn't they once saved the Crown Jewels together?

This should be a doddle!

3

Who *is* HD?

Vince grabbed the *Herald*. The editor had promised his advert would be published today.
It was!

A ROYAL DAY

Spend Griswold's Day in the gracious surroundings of the Royal Castle

PICNIC AREA

TEAS

LUNCH

MANY EXCITING ATTRACTIONS

Vince showed it to the King.

"On your own head be it," was the response.

"Mum?"

The Queen looked up from her book.

"Yep?"

As Vince passed her the paper, he caught sight of a headline on the letters page.

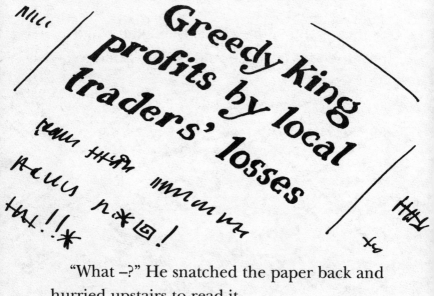

"What –?" He snatched the paper back and hurried upstairs to read it.

The letter accused the King of robbing hard-working folk; of taking business, it said, from the people who usually provided attractions on public holidays.

24

It was signed 'HD'.

Immediately, Vince took some paper and wrote:

Dear HD,

Have no fear. The people who provide entertainments have been invited to set up their attractions in the Royal gardens.

They'll earn good profits and help make the Castle Open Day a splendid occasion ~~for all~~ for all. I hope this puts your mind at rest.

Yours sincerely

Vincent (Prince)

He addressed an envelope. 'HD,' he began, then stopped. Who *was* HD? Ah! The newspaper editor would know – after all, HD must have seen the advertisement before it was published.

The editor flatly refused to reveal HD's identity. "I'll deliver your letter to him myself, Your Highness," he offered. "Best I can do."

Relieved, Vince headed home for a toasted sandwich with Larky, who was full of money-making ideas. So was Mrs Doughboy. She offered to ask her cousin with a gift shop about 'His Majesty' tea towels and 'Her Majesty' bookmarks.

"And 'His Highness' boxer shorts?" Larky suggested.

Vince grinned. "A tape of Larky singing? People could use it to scare birds off their seeds."

Macclesfield appeared with a silver tray. "Letter for you, Your Highness." He produced a brass paper knife.

"I'll do that!" Vince grabbed it. "Don't want
any accidents, do we?" The envelope was
splotched with yellow blobs. "Yuk!" He slit it
with the knife and took out the letter.

'Your Royal Highness,' he read to himself.

'Your royal letter does *not* put my mind at
rest.

28

You're heading for right royal trouble. I've got a living to make, so lay off. This is your final warning. HD.'

Vince disappeared up to his room to think. Who *was* HD?

The door burst open and a small shaggy dog scampered in.

Goofer!

Larky wasn't allowed up here, so she always sent her dog ahead and, if caught, pretended to be searching for him.

She made what was, for her, a stealthy entrance. "I saw your face when you got that letter," she announced. "What's up?"

Vince showed her. "It's kind of threatening. I must find out who sent it."

Larky's sniff was like a blast from a vacuum cleaner. "It's threatening, all right." She fished the envelope out of the bin and examined it. "No stamp," she pronounced.

"So?"

"So – it came by hand. Let's find out who brought it."

"Hordinary sort of chap, Prince Vincent, sah!" was Captain Boxer's unhelpful reply.

"No distinguishing marks?"

"No, sah! Hordinary round face, hordinary round body, hordinary baldy head, hordinary hot dog van –"

"Yeek!" Larky yelped, making Boxer's moustache quiver. "I know who HD is. He's –"

"Who?" Vince demanded.

"HD is – Hot Diggory!"

Vince's face cleared. "Of course! He owns all those hot dog vans. Hot Diggory's Hot Doggeries. They're everywhere."

"Specially weekends and holidays," said Larky. "You'd better sort this out, Prince Vince." She gulped. "Anyone who crosses Hot Diggory is dead meat!"

Diggory Dell

Vince frowned. "I'll have to talk to Hot Diggory and put things right." He opened the gate.

"I've got spuds to peel," said Larky quickly and set off in the opposite direction.

"Hey! I need you," Vince said.

She slunk back. "OK, but Goofer's not coming. Hot Diggory would probably cook him." She pointed the dog towards the castle. "Din dins," she bellowed, and shoved him, like a toy car, up the drive.

As they hurried through town, Larky

explained about Hot Diggory. "My mum worked for him – for one day. He fired her for licking ketchup off her fingers after she'd filled the squirters. Called her a dirty thief. He's horrible – everyone knows that, but people need jobs, don't they?"

Ten minutes later, the smell of onions drew them to iron gates set in a high wall. A notice proclaimed

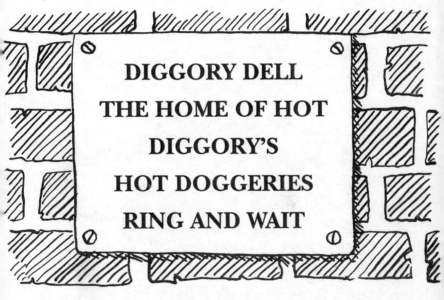

DIGGORY DELL
THE HOME OF HOT
DIGGORY'S
HOT DOGGERIES
RING AND WAIT

Larky shuddered as Vince pressed the bell. "Bet it's crawling with guard dogs."

A voice growled, "You rang?" A tough-faced attendant peered through the gate.

Vince nodded.

"What d'you want?"

"We want to see Hot Diggory."

The attendant opened the gate. "This way."

"What about the dogs?" Larky hissed to Vince.

"Probably locked up."

Her eyes widened. "*Probably*?!"

The attendant spun round. "Don't shout." He led them to a brilliant white building, topped by a blazing orange neon sign.

The onion smell was overpowering.

Inside, they blinked. Everything gleamed. Glossy worktops reflected silver machinery. Workers with flashing knives skinned onions and tossed them, whole, on to a moving conveyor belt which carried them up, up towards the ceiling.

Vince, head back, watched the onions. The conveyor jiggled them the length of the factory and tipped them down a slope into the smaller of two circular containers which whirled like cement mixers, crashing and grinding.

"Slicer," a worker explained. "The bigger one's the Meat Masher."

A series of tubes continued from the Masher into a vast white trough, into which tumbled hot dog sausages, plop, plop, plop.

Larky stared. "They're –"

"– dog-shaped!" said Vince. The sausages reminded him of the twisted and knotted balloon animals he'd seen at a party.

"Ugh!" Larky made a face. "Eating those would be like eating Goofer."

Suddenly, the workers fell silent as the light from the doorway was blacked out by the huge figure of a man; a round man, with a round face, a round body and round fingers, like round fat sausages.

Hot Diggory!

"Who have we here?" he boomed.
"Admiring my products?" He indicated a large board, illustrated with dog-shaped hot dogs.

"Try one, little miss."

Larky glowered.

"A Pierre Poodle, with French mustard? No? A Chi Chi Chihuahua, perhaps, with chilli sauce?" He saw her expression. "Too spicy? Try this." He opened a cabinet and swiftly concocted a hot dog. "The Chew Chin Chow, with sweet and sour sauce. Here!"

Larky, looking sick, accepted it.

"For you, sir," Hot Diggory continued, "the Bertie Bulldog. English mustard. Nice and hot."

Vince hadn't eaten since breakfast. He bit the head off his hot dog, ignoring Larky's scowl.

She held hers at arm's length. "Skusting!"

Vince remembered to introduce himself. "I'm Prince Vincent," he began, mouth still full.

Hot Diggory froze, then turned his back and flung a hunk of meat on to another conveyor belt. The meat began its journey, up, up, around, and down the slide – flump! – into the Masher, to be chewed and ground and scrunched by the sword-sharp choppers.

"Please," said Vince. "Can we talk?"

Hot Diggory jerked his head towards the door.

Larky followed them both outside. "What about the guard dogs?"

Hot Diggory looked sly. "You're safe with me." He turned to Vince. "I can't imagine you've anything of interest to say, Your Royalness."

"Why are you upset about Open Day?"

Hot Diggory grew red. "I'm upset, Your Royalty, because my Hot Doggeries always attend every fair or street party or picnic area on public holidays. Think about it, if you've half a royal brain. Suppose everyone spends Griswold's Day in your royal castle? I wouldn't sell a single hot dog, would I?"

"And that would never do," said a worker, emerging to dump gristle in a bin. "The money the boss makes on Griswold's Day pays for his annual holiday with his missus, don't it...?" Her voiced trailed away.

"Mind your own business," Hot Diggory

barked, "or I'll chuck you in the Masher." The worker paled. "If you don't get back to work," Hot Diggory roared, "I'll – I'll set the vicious guard dogs on you!"

The worker recovered. "But –" Then, seeing Hot Diggory's threatening gesture, she scuttled inside.

"What are you grinning at, Your Royalness?" Hot Diggory snarled.

"If that's all that's bothering you, forget it. You'll make your money."

Hot Diggory grabbed Vince by the collar. "How?" he snarled.

Vince nodded. "Simple. I need to speak to one person, just one, then we'll have a deal. No problem."

Larky groaned. She'd heard Vince say that so often.

It always led to trouble.

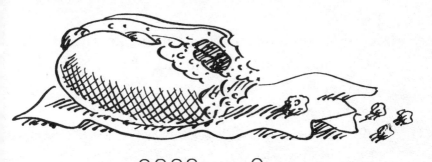

Who's Cooking?

Vince found the King in the Royal Games Room, pretending to repair the model railway. Everyone knew he was having a jolly good play, but pretended they didn't. That was best.

"Dad, can Hot Diggory do the catering for Open Day? Supply all the food? So he won't lose the profit he usually makes on Griswold's Day?"

The King shrugged. "Fine."

Vince felt relieved, but mean at the same time. Mrs Doughboy would be mad at being made redundant for the day. Still, as long as it was the King's wish, she wouldn't do anything drastic.

'Wish' was a bit strong. Better make sure; his dad was rather preoccupied. "That's your *wish* then?"

"I told you. Fine."

Vince was about to leave when the King added, "as long as Mrs Doughboy doesn't mind."

"I'm telling you, if she ever decided to leave I'd –"

Vince didn't stay to find out what. He hurtled downstairs, rehearsing the best way to break the news to Mrs Doughboy - without upsetting her.

He reckoned he could manage that.

Mrs Doughboy slammed down her wooden spoon. "Are you telling me as how the King wants Hot Diggory's hot dog vans in his gardens, selling that – *dog* food?"

"Only for one day, Mrs D. It'll make life easier for you." Vince reached for a cherry tart, but she brought the wooden spoon down sharply across his knuckles.

"If I'm good enough to cook for a King," she said, her face as stiff as a cliff, "I'm good enough to cook for anyone. I'd sooner leave than have that jumped-up sausage maker selling his junky rubbish on Royal ground. In fact –" she swept off her apron, "– that's exactly what I will do."

She headed for the stairs. "I'm going to give in my notice," she snapped, "to the King himself."

"No! Wait! Forget I mentioned it." Vince looked forlorn. "Give *me* a chance to put things right. Please."

She pretended to clip his ear. "Get on with you, then."

Vince had no choice. If Mrs Doughboy left, the King would go berserk, and Vince would be deemed a failure for ever.

"Larky, I've got to tell Hot Diggory the deal's off. Come with me," he begged.

"No way! He'd set the dogs on us," she retorted. "I'd write to him if I were you."

So Vince wrote a note of explanation,

ending, 'Regretfully yours, and hoping this won't cause any problems.'

"I'll take it myself," he said, and set off for Diggory Dell.

Twenty minutes later, he passed the letter to the attendant at the gate. "Please give this to Hot Diggory."

"Right away. D'you want to wait for a reply?"

"No!" said Vince hurriedly. "And there's no need to rush." He needed time to get away.

"Hey!" Hot Diggory's coarse voice shouted out. "Who's there?"

Vince ran!

He didn't stop running until he reached the castle gates. Just as he thought he was safe, a Hot Doggery van executed a skid stop behind him, spraying gravel over the guard, who barked, "Come 'ere, you nasty little 'ot dog person, you."

Vince slammed the gate shut, and leaned against it, panting.

The driver, a girl with purple hair, yelled, "Present from Hot Diggory," and flung a paper-wrapped package over the gate.

"His latest creation, designed specially for you.
It's called the Dirty Dog."

As Vince reached for the package, a
piercing voice yelled, "*Watch out!*"

Larky was haring up the drive.

Vince jumped aside, too late. Goofer
crashed into his knees as he scrabbled for the
hot dog.

The driver shrieked with laughter, spun the van round and roared away.

Vince wrestled the hot dog from Goofer.

"Let him have it," Larky said indignantly. "You won't eat it."

"This hot dog," Vince said dramatically, "could be poisoned."

She turned pale. Her mouth opened and closed soundlessly.

"The worst's over, though, Larky. Hot Diggory knows he's had it. This Dirty Dog was his parting shot."

She examined it. "So it might be pois-" She looked closer. "Hang on. There's writing on the paper."

Vince snatched it, brushed the dirt off the wrapper and read,

IF YOU THINK YOUR ROYAL open Day's going to ruin my summer holiday, you royal person, think again. Hot Diggory's not beaten

He screwed it up. "Nothing to worry about, Larky. What can he do?"

"Anything he likes."

"Rubbish," said Vince. "He can't do anything, as long as he doesn't get past the gate on Open Day. Come on. At least we can tell Mrs Doughboy she's doing the catering, without a hot dog in sight."

And so, Vince got on with his task, satisfied that he could safely put Hot Diggory right to the back of his mind.

Larky, however, wasn't so sure.

Ready

And what a task! Vince drew plans showing where the various attractions should be set up. He took care not to make mistakes, like putting the bouncy dragon near the archery competition.

He had a million things to remember.

"Keep the noise away from my Rest Room," warned the King.

"Don't let no strangers into ma library," said the Queen, who was still into Westerns. "Specially none of them kids. Sticky varmints."

Vince knew that if he was to come out of

this appearing halfway competent, nothing must be damaged or – heaven forbid – stolen!

He arranged for staff to be stationed in areas open to the public, and guards were to man a checkpoint at the exit to investigate large bags or suspiciously bulging coats. Boxer proved perfectly happy to help, as long as the Prince took overall responsibility.

"Fear not, Sah!" he assured Vince. "The Royal knick-knacks will be safe as 'ouses."

Vince certainly hoped so.

On the day before the opening, the castle
occupants were invited to a free afternoon at
the fair. The Queen spent the whole session
on a black roundabout horse, yelling, "Yee-
haaar!" and lashing her mount with her hat.

Larky was furious when Vince dragged her away from the fun to help check everything was in order. She groaned, like a hippo with toothache. "We've *done* it. A hundred times!"

"Once more. The fair's closing now, anyway."

They inspected the tour route. Private areas were cordoned off with thick velvety red ropes, and signs said

THIS WAY →

or

NO ENTRY

In the gallery, they met the King looking pleased as he surveyed his domain.

"Well, Vincent, I must admit –" he began, just as Larky dropped a curtsey. Unfortunately, she made rather a production of it, rolling off her heels to thud on the floor with a gasp that bounced around the walls.

Instead of complimenting Vince, the King glowered and shook his head. "Useless boy." He ambled downstairs.

"Larky, how could you!?" said Vince. "He was just going to say something nice. Hey, look at Mum!"

The Queen had returned from the fair, wearing earphones and a faraway expression. She whirled a feather duster like a whip.

Larky gaped. "What's she doing?"

"Listening to a story tape. Let's follow her."

In the library, the Queen flicked her feather duster over the books, yelling "Git on up, y'ornery critter."

"At least she's helping," Larky grunted.

"Waste of time." Vince indicated a notice on the door, saying, 'NO ENTRY'. "Let's check the kitchen."

Bowls of home-made strawberry jam stood ready, and tummy-rumbling smells wafted from the ovens. Mrs Doughboy slapped both their hands, Royal and otherwise, for pinching icing from her newest creation, Gâteau

Griswold. She gave them a lolly and sent them out.

The gardeners had worked overtime, and the grounds were beautiful. Everywhere they looked there were exciting stalls and activities; tombolas, pony rides, pets corner, the octopus – Vince's insides nearly burst with pride.

"This time tomorrow," he said, "it'll all be over."

Larky slurped juice from her fingers. "Except for the fireworks."

"What? There aren't going to *be* any fireworks."

"Hah!" said Larky. "There are if Hot Diggory turns up!

Hot Diggory
Attacks

Vince woke and looked out to a blue-gold morning.

Corks! People were already queuing!

By the time he was dressed and outside, it was almost ten. He signalled to Captain Boxer. Open up!

The crowd, slightly overawed, entered in an orderly fashion. Vince welcomed the first fifty or so personally.

Boxer approached him. "Sah! Lot of talk about mementoes, Sah!"

Vince nodded. "There's a souvenir shop in

the conservatory. Should make lots of money!"

"Beg pardon, Sah! Sounds more like freebies they're on abaht!"

Vince hesitated. "Don't be silly."

"No, Sah!"

Freebies? What was going on? Vince decided to investigate.

"Welcome," he said to an elderly man. "Do visit the souvenir shop."

"Shop be blowed," said the man. "I'm not buying nowt. I'm here for my free memento. Like he said." He jerked his thumb towards the entrance.

Vince went to the gate for a closer look. Just outside, a white van was parked. The orange sign on top said

HOT DOGGERY

and, handing out leaflets from the serving hatch was – Hot Diggory himself.

"Don't forget your free memento of your royal visit to their Royal Royalnesses royal castle!" he shouted.

Vince glanced wordlessly at Boxer.

"Can't stop 'im, Sah! Outside Royal grounds."

"Get me a leaflet," Vince ordered.

Boxer seized one from a woman and handed it to Vince, who read it out.

HAPPY OPEN DAY
FROM
THEIR ROYALNESSES
SELECT YOUR FREE
MEMENTO FROM THE
SELECTION DISPLAYED ON
THE TOUR ROUTE

Corks! All the King's precious possessions, the Royal valuables, the Queen's books...

Vince tore to the castle, only to meet a portly man staggering from the front door under the weight of the breakfast room fire screen.

"That's not yours!" Vince cried.

The man couldn't see round the screen. "Tis now, mate. You get your own bloomin' memento."

This was terrible. People were wandering out with ornaments that had been in the Royal family for hundreds of years. Vince had to stop them! If the King should appear...

A statuette was borne away by two men. "I want one of those," said a woman, clutching her leaflet.

The leaflets! Vince raced down the drive, through the gate and, before Hot Diggory knew what was happening, snatched the leaflets and headed back. Seeing a notice pinned to a tree –

WHEN YOU'VE GOT YOUR ROYAL FREEBIE – COME AND TRY OUR NEW 'BOXER DOG'

– he gritted his teeth and tore it down. That's enough of your tricks, he thought, without a backward glance.

But Hot Diggory was watching him. Smiling.

Vince was at the boating lake when he heard, over the music and shouts from the fair, even over the bangs from the shooting range, an ear-splitting bellow.

"Prince Vince!" Larky waved frantically. "In the castle, quick!"

He chased after her.

"There are notices *everywhere*," she shouted.

"I know. I put them up."

"Not these you didn't."

The first fake notice, on the library door, said

PICNIC AREA
FOR THOSE WHO
DON'T LIKE
DAMP GRASS
AND
ROYAL WASPS

Vince looked inside and nearly passed out. Visitors had spread picnic rugs on the floor and made themselves seats with the thickest books. There was the drainy smell of egg sandwiches; even a kettle boiling on a camping stove.

"Suffrin' polecats!" The Queen pushed
Vince out of the way, yanked out her
earphones and whirled them around her
head. "Garn!" she yelled. "Vamoose, pack
of...!"

She went unheard in the hubbub. Vince
took her arm. "Leave it to Larky." He and the
Queen ducked outside, fingers in their ears,
and waited. Seconds later, a torrent of people
poured out, fists full of sausage rolls and cake.

"Lemme out of here!"

"Gawd, what a racket!"

Larky emerged last. "All clear, Your
Majesty."

"Thank you kindly. And quit hollerin'."

Seeing Larky's hurt expression, Vince said,
"Show me the other notices."

They covered the castle, removing notices
offering nappy changing facilities in the King's
private loo, and an invitation to try on the
Crown Jewels - there were notices everywhere.

Outside the Royal Rest Room, Vince ripped
off a poster announcing 'Kiddies' Play Room'
and put his hand over Larky's mouth. "Shh."

He opened the door. "Dad?"

The King sat surrounded by heaps of knotted fishing line.

"Have you had a look at what's going on?" Vince asked, dreading the reply.

The King shook his head. "Later. Want to get this untangled. Meaning to do it for ages. Like a cup of tea though."

Larky boomed from the corridor, "I'll get it, Your Majesty." She galloped away.

The King jumped. "What was that?"

"Larky."

"Oh. Her. Always seems to be a kerfuffle when she's about." He frowned. "Don't tell me there's trouble with this Open Day. If you've messed up my castle I'll –"

"Everything's fine." Vince raced to the kitchen, in time to see Mrs Doughboy fling a dish cloth at Larky.

"*Course* I'm upset," she snapped. "Nobody's buying my lovely food, so *course* I'm upset."

Vince stared. "Nobody?"

"Almost nobody," said Mrs Doughboy. "Seen the tea room? My Royal Shorties, unsold. My Castle Cupcakes cluttering up the counter."

"Some people brought picnics," Vince explained. "We couldn't stop them."

"I know," she said, "but they didn't *all*." She pulled off her apron and flung it at Larky, who wore a 'why me?' expression.

"That's it." Mrs Doughboy blew her nose. "If my food's not wanted, I might as well go."

"Wait!" said Larky. "Perhaps – perhaps the Tea Room signs have fallen down, eh, Prince Vince? We'll check, won't we?"

Vince thought they'd better do something. If Mrs Doughboy left, the King - well, it didn't bear thinking about.

They hurried back outside, and stopped, aghast. Hundreds and hundreds of paper cups and napkins littered the gardens.

"What's happened?" Vince was staggered. "Where's it come from?"

A used napkin, orange, with black printing, blew against his ankle. He picked it up and read

"Look!" Larky pointed to the garden railings. "That's why nobody's buying Mrs Doughboy's food!"

Pepper

Stationed right round the edge of the
grounds, beyond the railings, was Hot
Diggory's whole fleet of Hot Doggeries. They
were selling hot dogs, from the outside, to the
visitors on the inside.

And Vince could do nothing about it.

He and Larky, under cover of a rose hedge,
spied on the nearest hot dog seller, the purple
haired girl.

"There you go, mate," she told her
customer. "Chuck the paper away after. The
King's hydrangeas won't know themselves next

year. Ooh, he *will* be pleased!"

"Larky, if Dad sees this litter... Quick, tell Boxer to get his men to pick-"

Hearing a cry of pain, he spun round. "Macclesfield! What's happened?"

The butler hopped painfully. He carried a long park-keeper's spike and his shoes were riddled with holes. "Trying to cope with the litter, Prince Vince," he said. "A poor shot, I fear."

"I'll do it," said Vince. "You get some plasters from the Queen."

Macclesfield hobbled away and Vince gazed round helplessly. The grounds were a shambles, Mrs Doughboy was on the point of leaving and the King might appear at any moment.

He didn't know which way to turn.

Larky's arms were already full of litter. "Why do they eat those disgusting things?"

"Taste, I suppose."

"I'll give them taste," she fumed. "I'd put something in those hot dogs that would –"

Vince dropped his spike. "Brilliant! Quick

– follow me!"

In the kitchen, Mrs Doughboy, grim-faced, was packing her knives and omelet pan.

"Trust me," Vince begged. "It'll be OK. Where's the pepper?"

She gave him a small china pot.

"No," said Vince. "More. More pepper. *Much* more."

"Help yourself," said Mrs Doughboy. "In the pantry."

"I'll get it." Larky fetched a large container, like a drum, labelled 'White Pepper'.

"Let's go," said Vince.

On the way, he told Larky his plan. "Go to each Hot Doggery in turn and be an awkward customer."

"What – me?"

"Yes. I might be recognised. You *must* keep the hot dog seller occupied. Start with the purple girl."

Vince slipped out through the gates to the rear of the van, while Larky queued at the serving hatch. When her turn came, she peered through the railings. "What you got?"

"Hot dogs. Hurry up, people's waiting."

"What sort of hot dogs?"

"Pierre Poodles," the girl recited, "Dieter Dachshunds, Chew Chin Chows –"

"Have you got a Sheep Dog?" Larky watched Vince, through the opposite window, as he opened the drum. Keeping his head to one side, he scooped out a handful of pepper. Larky snapped her attention back to the girl.

"Let's see," she said slowly. "I want –"

Vince screwed up his eyes and blew. A great cloud of pepper blasted into the van.

"*What* do you want?"

"A British Bulldog."

The girl stuffed a fat dog-shaped sausage into a roll, and sniffed, twice. She wiggled her nose.

Vince and Larky eyed each other.

The girl dropped the mustard squeezer and rubbed her nose frantically then, just as she passed the hot dog to Larky - "Ah - aah - aaah - *choooo*!"

All over the British Bulldog.

"Bleeuch!" Larky screeched. "Greeugh! Look what she's done. She's made a *Snotty Dog*!"

The crowd backed away in disgust. The purple-haired girl was sneezing so hard she didn't know what was happening.

"My kid's not eating *her* hot dogs," said a woman. "Let's try the next van."

Vince met Larky at the gates. "Hurry – same again."

They repeated the pepper trick at each van and, within half an hour, the queues had dispersed and people were drifting towards the castle in search of food.

Vince surveyed the garden. "Let's finish clearing the litter, Larky," he said, "then I think we can say we've saved the day."

He was picking up the last few paper cups when a hand gripped his shoulder.

"Where's my cup of tea?"

"My fault, King," said Larky. "We've been busy."

"Never mind." He glanced around. "Not bad, my boy. Visitors quite happy, nothing *seems* to be missing or damaged, and not much mess." He shook his head in wonder.

Vince's grin vanished as tyres screamed to a stop and Boxer shouted, "not allowed in! Royal command. Be orff!" He slammed the gates shut.

Hot Diggory leapt from his van. "I can't turn my back for a minute! Where is he? Where's the royal troublemaker?" He spotted Vince. "You!" he bellowed, shaking his fist through the gate. "You've ruined my trade – you've dirtied my clean vans and you've destroyed my good reputation." His frenzied voice rose even higher. "I'll give you Snotty Dogs!"

The King rounded on Vince, who was struck dumb by the tirade. Larky slunk behind a conker tree. "You appear to have upset this gentleman, Vincent. I suppose you'd like *me* to sort out your mess?" He strolled across to the gate. "Now, see here, my good man –"

"I'm *not* your good man, and he's been warned. He's gone too far, so now I'm warning *you*, Your Royal King. You've stopped me feeding the people. Now I'll stop the people feeding *you*!"

Dogs?
What Dogs?

"I've got power," Hot Diggory ranted. "I'll stop all the shops and factories from supplying you - you'll have no food, no milk, no coal - *nothing* will be delivered to your castle from now on."

"Remember who you're talking to, my man," the King blustered.

"He's not your man," Vince reminded him.

"*Shut up!*"

79

Vince joined Larky behind the tree.

"We've an excellent kitchen garden," said the King.

"Then you can live on turnips," sneered Hot Diggory. "I'll starve you, so you'll know what it's like to do without." He sniffed. "Like Mrs Diggory's got to do without her holiday." Shaking his fist, he strode away.

The King addressed the conker tree. "As I was saying, you've done it. You've *really* done it now! I should have known." He wheeled round. "Boxer!"

Vince felt sick.

"What will you do now?" Larky's penetrating whisper carried to where the King stood with the Captain.

"He'll do nothing, young lady," the King roared. "He's done quite enough already, so now he can leave this mess to someone more experienced. Hot Diggory won't get the better of *me*."

But he did.

At breakfast next morning, there was no milk.

"Not delivered today, Your Majesty," said Macclesfield.

At tea time, the King had to do without his evening paper and, next morning, when the toilet roll situation became critical, he sent Boxer to make peace with Hot Diggory.

The Captain returned before breakfast was over. "Beg pardon for distarbin' the Royal poached egg, Sah!" he said. "Went to make peace with 'ot Diggory as hinstructed. He wouldn't listen. Sah!"

The Queen made a face at her milkless tea. "Bitter as rattlesnake stew," she muttered. "I'd take a posse and bring him in."

"We don't want him *in*," said the King. "We want him sweetened up, so he won't starve us *out*."

Vince cleared his throat. "Actually, I've been thinking."

Boxer's nose swooped skywards.

"Vincent," said the King. "Don't think."

The Prince was fed up. Everyone thought he was useless. Well, he'd *do* something. He would.

First, he searched for Larky.

She heard him out, then laughed in disbelief. "You want me to go to Diggory Dell with you?"

"Please," said Vince. "I've got a proposition for Hot Diggory. It's so good he can't refuse."

"*If* he'll see you," she said. "And why must I go?"

"You'll find out. And bring Goofer."

Vince rang Hot Diggory's bell again and again. No one came.

Larky held tight to Goofer. "He won't see us."

"If we go to the factory he'll have to."

"With guard dogs everywhere? You're barmy, Your Highness."

To her horror, Vince started to climb the gate. "What dogs?" he demanded. "Did you ever see any dogs?"

"Well - no."

"Exactly. I don't think there are any."

"But what's the wall for," asked Larky, "if it's not to keep the dogs in?"

Vince perched astride the gate. "I don't believe it's to keep dogs in - I believe it's to keep dogs out."

Hot Diggory Dog

Vince burst into the factory, almost crashing into Hot Diggory who roared in fury. "Out!"

His workers made for the door.

"Not you, fools!" stormed Hot Diggory.

"Let them go," said Vince. "I've a proposition you might like."

Hot Diggory folded his arms over his bulbous stomach. "I *won't* like your proposition, and I'm not listening to it, so take your royal carcass out of here. Get lost!"

Bang. Thump. Click. He switched on all the machinery, plugged his fingers in his ears and shut his eyes.

"Please listen!" Vince begged.

"La! La-la! La-la!" Hot Diggory sang.

"If you don't listen," Larky blasted, "you'll be very, very sorry."

Hot Diggory pretended not to hear.

At Vince's signal, Larky bellowed from the doorway, "Gooo-fer! Goofer-oofer-oofer! Come here, you little scallywag, you!"

Goofer whirled into the factory, excited by the noises and smells.

Hot Diggory sang on, eyes shut, so Larky pointed Goofer towards him. "Play time! Go gettim!"

Goofer circled his quarry, barking. *Now* Hot Diggory saw him. He unplugged his ears, fast, and scrambled for the safety of the onion-chopper's work top. Goofer, wanting to play, tried to jump after him.

Hot Diggory's terrified yells drowned the noise of the machinery, and now Vince knew he'd guessed right.

Hot Diggory was petrified of dogs! No wonder the workers had given him funny looks when he'd carried on the pretence of having guard dogs.

Larky helped Goofer on to the work top.
"Play time! Go gettim, boy!"

Hot Diggory, sliding on slimy onion skins,
launched himself on to the conveyor belt that
carried onions to the Slicer. Goofer followed,
yapping happily.

His quarry, frightened of being shredded,
clambered across to the meat conveyor, which
carried him up, clear of the Slicer.

Larky lifted Goofer down to safety, while
Vince flicked off all the switches except two.
The ones he left on were the brake lever,
labelled Meat Conveyor, and the bright red
knob, labelled Meat Masher. The machinery
noise died to just a low hum from the
conveyor that carried Hot Diggory round just
below the ceiling.

All the time, the Meat Masher ground on.

Hot Diggory scrambled to his knees,
wobbling, and raised his fists in triumph.
"Can't reach me here, dog," he taunted.

Larky chased after him with a mustard squirter. "*I* can!" She aimed well. Yellow gobbets slopped down Hot Diggory's front as he travelled diagonally across the factory to the far corner. From there he would begin the long slope towards the Masher.

"And for my next trick," Vince chanted, "I will produce, with the aid of the Amazing Meat Masher, not a Boxer Dog, not a Sweet and Sour Dog, not even a Dirty Dog! I will produce the first, the one and only – **Hot Diggory Dog**!

"Noo-ooo-ooo-OOO!" came his victim's panic-stricken wail, as he realised the ghastly fate awaiting him. His arms thrashed wildly, bursting a plastic ketchup container which exploded in his lap. The conveyor tilted him forward and took him down the slope towards the Masher's gnashing choppers. "Stop! I'll listen!"

Larky stood wide-eyed with horror.

Vince pulled the brake lever.

The conveyor stopped with a jerk and shot Hot Diggory head first down the slope. He scrabbled in the red and yellow mess, desperate to get a hand or foothold, but in vain.

With a scream, he tumbled off the conveyor into the Masher.

In the split second before he landed, Vince slammed his hand down on the red knob. The Masher's choppers stopped and, with a sickly squelch, Hot Diggory vanished.

For a moment, all was still. Then, from inside the Masher, a round, slimy, spattered face slowly rose into view.

Goofer licked his lips.

Hot Diggory sighed. "I'm listening!"

A week later, Vince brought his parents out to the podium.

"Not more tomfoolery," barked the King, who'd barely spoken to Vince since Open Day. "And what the dubbins is she up to?" he demanded, spotting Larky, with Goofer on a lead. "Seems to me she *helps* you mess things up."

Vince took a deep breath. "I've agreed with Hot Diggory not to hold any more Open Days –"

The King laughed. "Given in, you mean!"

"No! We held the Open Day to raise money for instruments-"

"And you failed," said the King. "We hardly made enough from that fiasco to buy a penny whistle, let alone a trumpet. And you've agreed – words fail me." He made to leave the podium.

"Wait!" said Vince. He waved a large yellow hanky, like a signal.

"What the dubbins –?" The King cocked his head, listening. "What's that racket?"

"It's not racket, Dad. It's music."

The King's toe tapped. "Nice."

Larky hollered, "*By the* LEFT – *qui-ick MARCH*!"

From around the corner of the castle appeared the Royal Marching Band, instruments gleaming, sounding as pure as liquid gold.

"I'll be doggoned," said the Queen.

The King gasped. "How –? What –?"

As the band drew near, Larky bellowed, "HALT!"

Now there was only the boom of the big drum which Captain Boxer pounded steadily.

Larky threw her head back, cupped her hands around her mouth and bawled, "NOW!"

Beyond the gates an engine revved, and a white and orange van, with a flag draped over the bonnet, sped towards them.

"Omigosh!" the King gasped. "It's him! It's Hot Diggory! What's he up to now? Guards! Guards!?" When no one moved, he tried to run, but Vince held him back.

The van skidded to a stop. Hot Diggory leaned out, his round face one big grin.

"Would Your Royal Majesty care to lift the royal flag?"

Warily, the King lifted the flag from the bonnet of the van to reveal a golden crown, beneath which was written in scarlet

BY ROYAL APPOINTMENT
TO THE ROYAL FAMILY
ROYAL HOT DOGGERIES

Vince grinned at his father's confused and horrified expression. "Look at the drum, Dad."

The King squinted. There was printing on it! He peered closer and read aloud

"See, Dad? If we don't hold any more Open Days, Hot Diggory will pay for the upkeep of the band. So everybody's happy."

The King was bewildered. "Everybody?"

"Not quite, Your Royalty." Hot Diggory clambered from his van. "Now I've paid for those instruments, there's *no* chance of Mrs Diggory having her expensive holiday." He glanced up at the castle. "I'm looking for somewhere cheap to take her. Just for the fortnight." He peered through a ground floor window. "I wonder..."

The King growled, "Vincent –?"

But Vince was prepared for trouble. He bent down, unclipped Goofer's lead and whispered, "play time...!"